Two eggs, please.

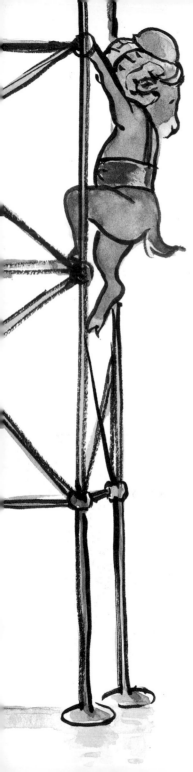

For the two new babies in town, Grace and McGhee

—S. W.

To John and Marie Simmons, a couple of good eggs.
Thanks to the Cheyenne Diner and to Lupeta,
who showed me how to hold eight plates at once

—B. L.

For all the "good eggs" at Cherry Tree!

Sarah Weeks

March 16, 2011

Two eggs, please.

written by
SARAH WEEKS

illustrated by
BETSY LEWIN

Atheneum Books for Young Readers • New York London Toronto Sydney Singapore

"Two eggs coming up!"

Different...

but the same.

Atheneum Books for Young Readers
An imprint of Simon & Schuster Children's
Publishing Division
1230 Avenue of the Americas
New York, New York 10020

Book design by Ann Bobco
The text of this book is set in Base Mono, Berliner Grotesk,
Blockhead, Bodega Serif, Cafeteria, Clicker, Comic Sans, and Meta.
The illustrations are rendered in watercolor and ink.
Printed in the United States of America
First Edition
2 4 6 8 10 9 7 5 3 1
Library of Congress Cataloging-in-Publication Data
Weeks, Sarah.
Two eggs, please. / Sarah Weeks ;
illustrated by Betsy Lewin.—1st ed.
p.   cm.
Summary: A look at the many different ways to prepare the very
same food, as everyone in a diner orders eggs.
ISBN 0-689-83196-X
[1. Eggs—Fiction. 2. Diners (Restaurants)—Fiction.]
I. Lewin, Betsy, ill. II. Title.
PZ7.W42215 Tw 2003
[Fic]—dc21   2002005291

Different.

The same.